One day, Paddington's friend Mr Gruber took him on a surprise outing to a part of London known as 'Little Venice'.

"It's called Little Venice because it's by a canal," he explained, "and every spring they hold a big Carnival. Boats come from all over the country to take part in the celebration."

Paddington always enjoyed his days out with Mr Gruber. He waved as one of the boats went past. All the people on board waved back.

"I've never been for a ride on a canal before," said Paddington.

"Who knows," said Mr Gruber mysteriously, "perhaps you will before the day is out. But first of all, we must see what else is happening. We don't want to miss anything important."

He pointed to a board showing all the different events, but there were so many, Paddington didn't know which to try first.

"How about the Busy Bee Adventure Trail?" suggested Mr Gruber. "You have to find as many things as possible beginning with the letter B."

Paddington thought that sounded like a very good idea, especially when Mr Gruber told him the first prize was a free boat ride for two.

"Bears are good at trails, Mr Gruber," he explained.

Looking around he could already see lots of things beginning with the letter B. Apart from B for BOARD, there was a BOY blowing BUBBLES, a man eating a BAGEL, and another with a BROOM, a BARBECUE, and a lady selling BANANAS. There were BOATS everywhere and lots of BALLOONS. There was even a man playing the BANJO in a BAND.

After Paddington had finished writing them all down, he and Mr Gruber set off along the canal.

In no time at all, Paddington had added five other items to his list: first there was B for BRIDGE, and then

BLACKBIRD,

BUTTERCUP,

BLOSSOM and

BUTTERFLY.

They hadn't gone very far
when they saw a lady
feeding some ducks.

She was wearing a
BONNET, a BLOUSE fastened
at the neck with a BROOCH, and around
her wrist she wore a BRACELET.

When she saw Paddington she smiled and said, "Would you like some?"

"Thank you very much," said Paddington. He wrote down BAG and BREAD. He then raised his hat politely and said, "Busy Bee Adventure Trails make you hungry."

"This is the sort of day out I like, Mr Gruber!" Paddington announced, as he took a jar of marmalade from his suitcase and began making a sandwich.

"Ahem, Mr Brown." Mr Gruber gave a cough. "I think you were really meant to give the bread to the ducks."

Before Paddington had time to reply, there was a loud buzzing noise and something landed on his marmalade.

Paddington gave the object a hard stare before adding BEE to his list.

Next, they came upon a man fishing.

"I think you've struck lucky, Mr Brown," whispered Mr Gruber.

He waited patiently while Paddington wrote down BOX, followed by BERET, BEARD, BELT, BUCKLE, BOOTS, BUCKET and BASKET.

"Would you like to have a try?" asked the man. "You can use some of my worms if you'd like."

Paddington thought that was a very good idea, but first he wrote down B for BAIT.

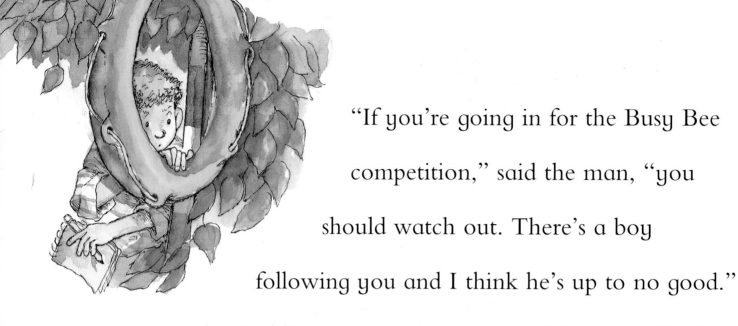

"If you're going in for the Busy Bee competition," said the man, "you should watch out. There's a boy following you and I think he's up to no good."

Paddington was about to say "thank you" when he felt a tug on the fishing line. "I think it might be too big to go in my jar, whatever it is!" he exclaimed. "It feels like a W for WHALE."

"I'm not sure you'll find any whales this far inland,

Mr Brown," said Mr Gruber tactfully.

All the same, to be on the safe side, Mr Gruber tied

some rope around his friend.

"Strike me pink!" said the fisherman. "It's a BICYCLE!"

Paddington was most disappointed.

"Never mind," said Mr Gruber. "At least it's another word for your list."

Shortly afterwards, they came upon a stretch of water with high banks and trees on either side. Paddington decided to have a go at riding the bicycle. But he soon discovered why it had been thrown away.

"I think I'd better hold the other end, Mr Gruber," he gasped, pointing to the rope still tied around his waist. "In case I fall in the canal."

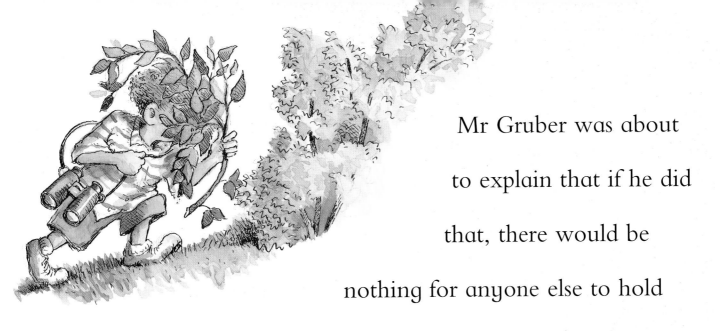

Mr Gruber was about

to explain that if he did

that, there would be

nothing for anyone else to hold

on to, when he saw the look on Paddington's face.

"Is anything the matter, Mr Brown?" he asked.

"I think we're being followed by a

B for BUSH, Mr Gruber,"

hissed Paddington.

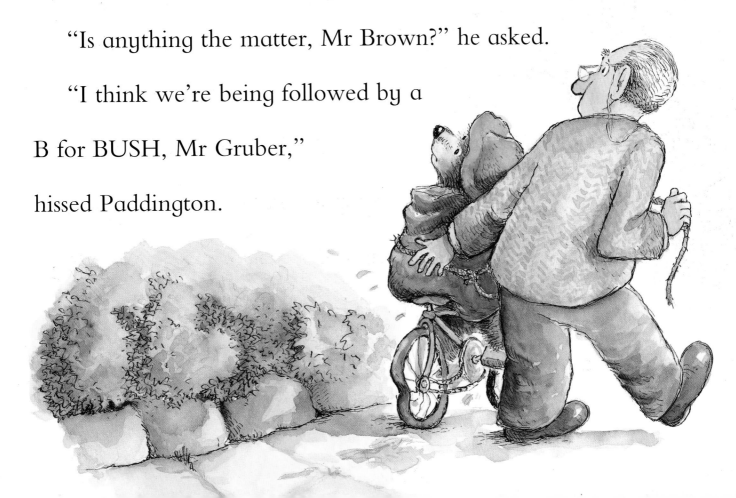

"Come back!"

shouted Mr Gruber.

"Whoever you are!"

Meanwhile, Paddington

added BINOCULARS to his list.

While he was writing, a boat went past and one

of the passengers had a BABY on her lap. She was feeding

him from a BOTTLE. The baby was wearing a BIB

and his sister was holding a BALL.

Mr Gruber sat down by the water while Paddington added up his list.

Altogether, with the BANK and BRAMBLES next to Mr Gruber, he had forty-one things beginning with the letter B.

Mr Gruber looked at his watch.
"I think it's time we got back,
Mr Brown," he said. "We don't
want to be late for the judging."

"Good luck," called the
fisherman as they went past.

"We shall be cheering you on," said the lady

feeding the ducks.

"Has anyone collected more than forty B's?" called the judge.

"I have!" cried Paddington, waving his piece of paper excitedly. "I've got forty-one."

"So have I!" came a voice from nearby.

Mr Gruber looked over the boy's shoulder. "This list is exactly the same as young Mr Brown's," he said sternly. "You must have been copying it word for word!"

"Oh dear," said the judge. "We can't have that. I'm afraid
I shall have to stop the contest!"

"It's all right, Mr Gruber!" called Paddington. "We've
won. I've thought of another B. That gives me forty-two."

"Fancy nearly forgetting the most important item of all," said Mr Gruber, as they set off on their boat trip. "What made you think of it?"

"I saw my reflection in the water," explained Paddington.

Mr Gruber nodded. "It's often the hardest of all to see things that are right under your nose," he said.

"It is if you're a B for BEAR," agreed Paddington. "Bears have very long noses."

It was dark by the time Paddington and Mr Gruber

arrived back, and the fireworks had already started.

Mr Gruber bought a packet of sparklers and, as they

stood on the bridge to watch, Paddington joined in with

his own display.

With his sparkler, he waved

Thank you Mr Gruber
for a lovely day out.

In the excitement, the only person who noticed

was Mr Gruber himself, but that was

really all that mattered.

"If you ask me, Mr Brown," said Mr Gruber, as they made their way home, "the nicest B of all is yet to come."

"I think I know what that is," said Paddington sleepily.

"It's B for BED!"